# THE WEATHER GIRLS

TO SEBASTIAN, MY DREAM CATCHER . . .

# THE WEATHER GIRLS

Aki

MACMILLAN CHILDREN'S BOOKS

Laura

Miffy

Annie

Rebecca

Jane

Vanessa

June

Melanie

# MEET THE WEATHER GIRLS

Sarah

Cathleen

Lucy

Zoe

Kirsten

Tilly

Joy

Emily

It's summertime. We rise and shine!

All set to go, we form a line.

A big, bright sun.

Let's have some fun!

We swim and dive and splash and run.

Lush green forest, fresh clean air.
Look at all the creatures there!

Autumn is windy in the city.
Trees are gold and red and pretty.

It's time for jumpers and for fun.

Through fallen leaves

we run and run!

We hop on bikes and ride and ride.

We pick apples
side by side.

Wintertime brings lots of snow.

Brrrr, brrrr, girls.

Let's go, go, go!

Through a blizzard, climb and climb.

The mountain's tall.

It takes some time.

The snow has stopped,

and we do, too.

The sky is big and bright and blue.

Spring is springing
through the trees.

We can feel the gentle breeze.

A big balloon!

Hooray,

hooray!

Up we go; we float away.

Strong winds blow...
We fly, fly, fly.

Now look up –

A rainbow sky!

# MEET THE SEASONS

Spring, summer, autumn, winter — the Weather Girls love them all!

# SUMMER

June, July, August

We see lots of animals out and about.

Plants are greenest. Temperatures are highest.

Days are longest. Sunshine is strongest.

# AUTUMN

September, October, November

We see fewer animals. Leaves change colour
and fall from the trees. Temperatures are cooler.

Days get shorter. There's less sunshine.

# WINTER
### December, January, February

Many animals hibernate or travel for warmer weather. Some trees and plants lose their leaves. Temperatures are coldest. Days are shortest. Sunshine is weakest.

# SPRING
### March, April, May

We start to see more animals. Trees and plants grow new leaves and become greener. Flowers bloom. Temperatures are rising. Days get longer. There's more sunshine.

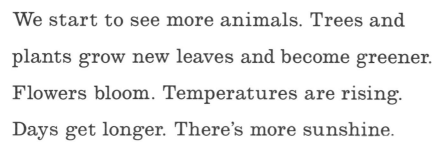

First published in the USA 2018 by Henry Holt and Company

First published in the UK 2018 by Macmillan Children's Books

an imprint of Pan Macmillan

20 New Wharf Road, London N1 9RR

Associated companies throughout the world

www.panmacmillan.com

ISBN (HB): 978-1-5098-7130-8

ISBN (PB): 978-1-5098-7131-5

1 3 5 7 9 8 6 4 2

A CIP catalogue record for this book is available from
the British Library.

Printed in Spain